Take Me To The Cliff

Kaci Rose

Copyright

Copyright © 2023, by Kaci Rose, Five Little Roses Publishing. All Rights Reserved.

No part of this publication may be reproduced, distributed, or transmitted in any form or by any means, including photocopying, recording, or other electronic or mechanical methods, or by any information storage and
retrieval system without the prior written permission of the publisher, except in the case of very brief quotations embodied in critical reviews and certain other noncommercial uses permitted by copyright law.

Publisher's Note: This is a work of fiction. Names, characters, places, and incidents are a product of the author's imagination. Locales and public names are sometimes used for atmospheric purposes. Any resemblance to actual people, living or dead, or to businesses, companies, events, institutions, or locales is completely coincidental.

Book Cover By: **KiWi Cover Design Co.**

Editing By: Debbe @ **On The Page, Author and PA Services**

DEDICATION

To all those who ever think of running off to the mountain and leaving everyday life behind, even just for a weekend.

Contents

Get Free Books!		IX
1.	Chapter 1	1
2.	Chapter 2	7
3.	Chapter 3	14
4.	Chapter 4	20
5.	Chapter 5	34
6.	Chapter 6	42
7.	Chapter 7	58
8.	Chapter 8	65
9.	Chapter 9	74
10.	Chapter 10	83
11.	Chapter 11	90

12. Epilogue 101

GET FREE BOOKS!

Do you like Military Men? Best friends brothers?
What about sweet, sexy, and addicting books?

If you join Kaci Rose's Newsletter you get these books free!

https://www.kacirose.com/free-books/

Now on to the story!

CHAPTER 1

JACK

I did it.

I can't believe I finally did it.

After all these years of watching the other mountain men come into my shop and sell their items it did it, I think enviously of their lifestyle up on the mountain.

As of yesterday, I officially own a cabin on the mountain as well. I moved everything in and today is the first time I get to really come home from town to my cabin.

Taking a minute, I admire it before heading inside. It needs some work and it'll be a few years before I'm truly self-sufficient out here, but I'm up for the task and I know Axel, Phoenix, Cash, Cole, and Bennett will have my back if I need anything.

Since it's so remote, I don't lock the door. Really, no one even knows this place exists out here. One of the reasons is because the driveway is really easy to miss if you don't know where to look. If I'm being honest, it was a huge part of its appeal.

When I enter, I'm surprised that the living room light is on. I don't remember leaving it on, but anything's possible. It was so quiet out here that I overslept and was in a rush to get out of the house this morning. Not only did I have to go in and check on the shop, but I needed to make sure that my old place was cleaned before I turned in the keys to my landlord.

My expectation is to set my keys down and start dinner. What I'm not expecting is the curvy brunette in sweatpants and a tank top with no bra to be sitting on the couch.

Fuck. She's gorgeous and I can almost see through her damn shirt. Who the hell sent her here? Whoever it was, they knew what they were doing because I'd follow her to hell just for a taste.

"What the hell are you doing here?" I ask her. Normally, I wouldn't think to cuss in front of a woman, but I am caught completely off guard.

"I could ask you the same thing. This isn't your cabin," she says, pulling the blanket off the back of the couch to cover herself.

"As of a couple of days ago, I can assure you that it is. Now again, who are you?" I widen my stance and cross my arms. I don't feel threatened by her, but I want to make it clear that I'm not playing around either.

I used to be a criminal lawyer and I know there are a lot of games that criminals will play, including sending in a beautiful young woman as a distraction.

"This is Greg's cabin. I was told I could use it anytime I want."

She's right, it was Greg's cabin but I just bought it from him last week. Greg is an old geezer who can't even make it up the mountain anymore. Also, why does her arguing with me have me hard as fucking nails?

"How do you know Greg?" I ask.

"He is my college roommate's uncle," she says.

Greg never had kids, but he was the oldest of ten kids, all of whom went on to have children of their own. The last time I talked to him, he had something like thirty-six nieces and nephews.

"Greg sold me this cabin last week. He was getting too old to come up here. You're going to have to find somewhere else to have your little woodsy vacation," I tell her ready to throw her out.

The last thing I need is some college kid thinking she can have a party up here with her friends. I wonder if Greg knew what the plans for his place were.

She stands and I think she's going to grab her stuff, but she looks around, folds the blanket back up, and sets it on the back of the couch where she got it. That's when I noticed the large bruise on her arm. The one in the shape of a handprint.

When she turns back to face me, it's clear tears are in her eyes and her jaw is wobbly.

"I'm sorry I bothered you. I didn't know he sold the place, and I needed to get away and figure a few things out. Just let me get changed and I'll get out of your way. Though I have no idea where I'm going to go," she sighs, walking off toward the hallway where the bedrooms are.

Hell, I shouldn't want a stranger in my house and certainly not as badly as I want her. Thinking over what she just said, I put the pieces together. She's hiding out from the person who put that bruise on her arm. Whoever she is hiding from sure as hell does not want to meet me or my friends, as we don't take too kindly to men putting their hands on women around here.

If I hadn't had to turn in my keys, I'd take her there and let her stay a few nights to get back on her feet. But that isn't an option now.

I don't need to be inviting this kind of trouble into my life, not now, not with everything going so well. But I also know I need to make sure that she is taken care of, and that she will be safe.

A few minutes later, she steps out in jeans and a sweater that hugs her curves. Dammit, if those curves aren't something I would ride to my death on.

There's a voice in the back of my head telling me I'd be a complete idiot to let her walk away right now.

Yet that's exactly what I planned on doing.

Chapter 2

Sage

I can't stay here with a guy I don't know, of course, I can't. Not even one that looks like this man here. The problem is, I have nowhere else to go. I can't go back to Mark. If I go back, I know the attacks will be worse. I saw it when my mom tried to leave her now ex. If you don't have a solid game plan, you can't get out.

Unfortunately, this was supposed to be my place to breathe and get a game plan in place. I have a semester left of college, but I got lucky one day when class was canceled and Mark was at work. I grabbed what I could and I left.

Think Sage, you need to figure this out because it will be way too cold to sleep in your car tonight. I can head into town and see if there is a hotel or B&B where I could stay. I'm sure there has to be something, even in this small town of Whiskey River, Montana.

Wiping my eyes because I don't want him to see me cry, I pack my bag, which isn't much, just what I was able to grab on my way out the door. I change out of my pajamas into jeans and a sweater, something that will help keep me warm until I figure out where I'm going. Then, taking a deep breath, I return to the living space.

He's still standing in the same place just inside the front door, but he's so big that it makes the space feel crowded. This isn't a huge cabin to begin with. I can tell from the windows just behind him that it's already starting to get dark and if I want to make it down the mountain while I still have daylight, I need to get going now.

"I'm really sorry for bothering you. I had no idea the cabin had been sold. Then again, I didn't tell anyone I was coming here either.

I just figured it would be safer that way," I say without really thinking. Then my next thought was I might have given too much away.

Hoisting the strap of my duffle bag over one shoulder and my purse and my backpack over the other, I walk past him toward the car I parked off to the side of the cabin. Even though I can feel his eyes on me the whole time, I don't bother looking as I go outside.

Then I open the backseat and set my bags inside before getting into the car. It isn't until I sit down in the driver's seat that I notice the man has stepped out on the porch and is watching me. Probably making sure I actually leave, not that I can blame him.

When I put the key in the ignition and turn it, there's nothing. Taking a deep breath, I do it again, but this time there's just a click, and that's it. I tried a third time and again there was nothing.

I rest my head on the steering wheel for just a moment. Of course, now would be the time my car finally dies on me. Opening the car door, I step back outside, facing the man on the porch.

"My car isn't starting," I sigh again, trying to run through my options.

I could sleep in my car tonight, but I'm pretty sure it's going to get below zero and since it's not starting that means I will have no heat. It's way too far to walk into town. And I didn't pass a single soul on the road up here, so I doubt hitchhiking is an option either.

"All right, I can take a look at it in the morning and see what it needs but I'm not going to be able to do much tonight," he pauses and looks off to the side into the woods before looking back at me. "You can stay here tonight and then tomorrow we'll go into town and get what you need for me to fix the car."

I really want to say no I'll figure it out, but as I don't really have any other options that don't lead to me freezing to death at some point tonight, I nod my head.

"What's your name?" I ask him, figuring if I am going to stay here, I should at least know the man's name.

"Jack. What's yours?"

"Sage. Thank you for letting me stay here tonight," I tell him. Then I grab my bag out of the back seat before hesitantly walking back to the cabin.

He holds the door open for me and I follow him inside. I set my stuff down on the couch, thinking I'll just sleep here out of the way.

I turn around in time to see a large shepherd dog coming through the door. The dog's fur is long and has splashes of white and black all over. When the dog sees me, she gets all excited and runs right over to me, sniffing.

"This is Sadie. During the day, she does her own thing but comes home in the evening. She's friendly, just don't feed her anything because she has absolutely zero table manners," he says with a smile.

"Okay, I'll just sleep here out of the way. I promise you won't even know I'm here," I tell him as I grab a throw pillow and pull the blanket off the back of the couch.

"Not a chance. My mama would kill me. You take the bed, Sadie, and I will stay out here. I've slept on this couch more times than I can count. Let me get ready for bed and then the room will be all yours."

"Oh, I can't kick you out of your own bed. The couch is absolutely fine," I tell him, shaking my head.

"Not an option and it's not negotiable," he says before strolling into the bedroom to get ready for bed.

While I'm waiting, I pet Sadie until he comes back out. He picks up my bag and carries it into the bedroom, putting it on the bed. I follow him and Sadie follows me.

"If you need anything, don't hesitate to wake me up. I'll keep the fire going in the fireplace and the house should stay relatively warm," he says but doesn't wait for an answer as turns and goes into the living room.

Sadie looks at me, then looks at him, and then looks back to me before jumping up on the bed and lying down.

"I guess you're staying with me, huh, girl?"

Chapter 3

Jack

I lie down on the couch and try to get as comfortable as possible with a throw pillow and the blankets that were on the back of the couch that now smells like her. Her scent on the blanket is making me hard, but I don't dare try to take care of myself, not with her in the next room.

Lying there, I see that the light under the doorway is on, but eventually, it's turned off and things are quiet. Sadie is in there watching over her as I lay here and think about my day. The bruise on her arm was definitely from someone grabbing her. It looked fresh too, not more than a day or two old.

Does she have bruises elsewhere? Is this bruise just one in a long line of them or was it the first one and she left? So many questions I'm desperate to know the answer to.

That's when I hear a whimpering sound. I stop and listen. Sage is crying quietly in the bedroom. Even though I know today didn't go as either of us planned, I'm not going to be able to take listening to her cry while I sit here on the couch.

Finally, I get up and make her a cup of hot cocoa before taking it into the bedroom. Knocking lightly on the door, I don't wait for anyone to answer as I crack open the door.

"A cup of cocoa makes everything look better. At least that's what my mom always used to say." She sits up in bed, wiping the tears from her face as Sadie snuggles up to her side.

"I'm sorry, I didn't mean to keep you awake," she sniffles before taking the cup from me and wrapping her hands around it.

"I was awake. It takes a little bit for me to fall asleep," I confess to her although I don't know why. "Do you want to talk about it?"

Though I ask her softly because if she is being abused as I suspect, I want her to know that I'm on her side even if I have the compulsive desire to rip whoever laid a hand on her from limb to limb.

"There's nothing really to tell. I tried to leave, and he was not happy," she shrugs like it's no big deal.

"You're crying because you guys broke up?" I ask, not liking the thought.

"No, that's not the reason. I called my mom, and she told me that I don't really have a choice. I need to go back to my ex, Mark." She takes another sip, eyeing me tearfully.

"Why don't you have a choice? You always have a choice," I tell her, getting extremely irritated. I've heard this song and dance before. In fact, I hear it all the time at the women's shelter.

Since the women don't feel like they have a choice, they go back to the abusive partner. Sometimes out of loyalty, but mostly because they just can't find a way to get out and make it on their own. They can't get a job or don't have enough money to get a place of their own, so they feel like they have no other options.

"I thought I had choices, and that's why I came up here to figure things out. But the truth is, I can't afford to get a place in town. Hell, I'll barely be able to afford to fix my car. So no, I don't have a choice. I'm going to try to get some sleep," she says, handing me back the half-filled cup of hot chocolate.

For a moment I hesitate because I feel like there's something that I should say to help her out, but I can't seem to find the words. So I walk to the doorway and pause again. This time she speaks.

"Besides, being with him is better than being alone. Anything's better than being alone." She then turns out the lights by the bed, but before I close the door, I reply.

"I always thought being alone was better than being miserable with someone else. But I can make myself happy. I don't need someone else to do it for me. If you need me, I'll be on the couch. Get some rest knowing that tonight you're safe here," I tell her. Then close the door behind me.

As a lawyer, I've dealt with domestic abuse cases. Back in the day when I was at a big shot law firm, I was charged with defending guys like her ex and making sure they didn't see jail time. I hated every minute of it.

It's why I eventually left the law firm to do pro bono work at places like the women's shelter. I want to help the true victims out and put guys like her ex behind bars where they belong. I don't want criminals to get away with doing anything they want, and I hate that our justice system works like that.

Before lying down on the couch again, I do a final check on the house, making sure all the windows and doors are locked and everything is closed up, and turning all the lights off.

Since I moved here, I've protected many women at the women's shelter a few towns away. While it's normal wanting to help someone and wanting to do good, but something about Sage feels different.

No, this is a compulsive need to protect her. It's a feeling, unlike anything I've ever felt in my life. She wants to leave tomorrow, but even though I moved up here with the intent of being alone, I don't think I can let her walk away.

At least I tell myself that I can't let her walk until I know that she's safe, but I know the feelings I have about it are much more than for her safety.

Chapter 4

Sage

I slept for shit last night. Even with the dog by my side and with Jack on the couch in the living room, I still jumped at any little noise. Every animal sound outside, I was sure it was Mark who had come to find me.

Every time the dog moved and shifted into another spot, I was certain she was getting up to attack someone trying to come into the room. It was only when the first rays of sunlight started to coat the sky outside the window that I finally closed my eyes and got a few hours of sleep.

Despite taking over his house, Jack lets me sleep in. After getting roughly three hours of sleep, the smell of coffee and bacon from the kitchen wakes me up. When I finally open my eyes, Sadie isn't in the room, so I guess he quietly let her out when he got up. Though I'm grateful that he let me sleep when he came and got her.

Using the attached bathroom, I get dressed in jeans and another sweater. There is no point in letting him see me in my pajamas again and putting the bruise that he questioned me about on full display. After brushing my hair and teeth and packing up my bag, I hesitantly walk out to the kitchen.

Since I'm invading his cabin, I didn't expect him to cook for me, and yet at the dining room table is a full meal of bacon, biscuits, and huckleberry jam, along with coffee. Taking a quick glance at him in the kitchen, I see he's cooking eggs on the stove.

"I hope I didn't wake you up. I was going to let you sleep until I was done cooking," he says with a huge smile on his face.

The smile is in contrast to the frown he wore pretty much all last night.

"Well, it smelled so good I think you could have woken the dead. But you really didn't have to cook for me. I'll be out of your way as soon as possible," I say.

He shakes his head. "I have to head into town anyway to check on my store, but I'll take a look at your car before we go and see if it's something I can fix. If so, we can grab the part and I can get it going. Unfortunately, with everything I have to make sure I get done while in town, chances are I won't be able to fix it until tomorrow. But that's only if I'm able to get the part in town."

My heart sinks because I have no place to go and I know he was only being nice, allowing me to stay here last night.

"I'm not going to throw you out in the cold, Sage. You're welcome to stay here, and in fact, I insist on it."

"But I don't want to be in the way. I know you hadn't planned on anyone being here," I tell him.

"Well, neither did you, so we can both just adjust our plans. It's not a big deal, I promise."

"Okay, as long as you're sure I'm not going to be a bother, I appreciate you letting me stay." At my words, I'm completely unprepared for the delighted smile that crossed his face once I agreed to stay.

"Take a seat at the table, I'm finishing up omelets now," he says.

When I sit down where he indicated, Sadie walks out of the kitchen and sits next to me, facing Jack as well. Not able to resist, I reach out and pet her. But she sits there as if she's standing guard.

"Was she okay in the room with you last night?" he asks, nodding to Sadie as he plates the omelets.

"Yes. If I'm being honest, it was nice to have her there. She made me feel safer."

"Good, then she will be sleeping with you while you're here. I want you to know that you are safe here because I will see to it," he says seriously.

Then he walks over and sets an omelet almost the size of my head down in front of me. My eyes widen when I see that his omelet is even bigger.

"Oh, this is no way that I can eat all of this."

"Eat what you can. Sadie will be more than happy to take care of the rest," he says. At the mention of her name, Sadie starts wagging her tail and getting all excited though she still doesn't move from her seated position watching us eat.

"You said you had to check on the shop. What kind of shop do you have?" I ask, trying to make conversation and fill the silence of the room.

"I own the Whiskey River Local Retail store downtown. It's part outdoor store for people going between Glacier National Park and Yellowstone National Park and part handmade items that are made locally. Other mountain men sell things they make

CHAPTER 4

for the store. Recently, their wives have begun selling things as well."

There are other mountain men, like Jack, in the area who are married? I think to myself. Usually, when I think of mountain men, I think of guys like Jack who lives in a cabin in the woods and stay to themselves.

Unlike Jack, I don't think they have air conditioning in their house or electricity, for that matter. I pictured guys that live completely off the grid that hardly ever go into town for anything. I definitely don't picture them having wives or families.

But imagining a life out here doesn't seem so bad. Away from people and noise. The whole reason I came out here was to be alone. To prove to myself that I could be alone, especially after what Mark said.

"Well, I can't wait to see it. I didn't get a chance to drive through downtown Whiskey River because I came in from the other end."

We finish our food, though I am only able to eat about half the omelet that he made along with biscuits, homemade jam, and several slices of bacon. True to what Jack said, Sadie was more than happy to finish the other half of my omelet. Jack gave her some biscuits and a piece of bacon, too. Once we were done, she happily went to the kitchen to stand guard in case any food should fall during clean up.

"Since you cooked, let me clean up while you get ready," I say.

He looks hesitantly at me.

"I know how to do dishes, I promise," I smile, trying to convince him that I can do this on my own.

"Okay, but just set everything in the drying rack and I will put them away when I'm done."

"Deal."

He heads into the bedroom to get his things and get ready, while I do the dishes. As I'm working on this mundane task, my mind starts to wander. I hadn't planned to visit the town of Whiskey River. Mostly because

CHAPTER 4

I didn't want anyone to know I was there. My college roommate told me about the town and how beautiful it was. She said it was one of her favorite places. When she was growing up and when her parents would allow it, she loved coming to the cabin with her uncle.

It's been a few months since we talked last, and God knows how long it's been since she talked to her uncle. So of course, I had no idea this place had been sold. I should reach out to her and see if she knows.

As I'm just finishing up the dishes, Jack steps out of his room, he's got on jeans, a t-shirt, an open flannel shirt, and boots. Yesterday when I saw him, he was dirty and had on really worn-out jeans and a long sleeve T-shirt which was threadbare and old.

Today, seeing him in jeans that fit, and the flannel that he's wearing, he looks sexy. Great, just what I need. Going from one man to the next. I need to stop looking at him like this, especially before he catches me.

Entering the kitchen, he dries the dishes and puts them away and I go over to sit on the couch and pet Sadie.

"Alright. Grab your keys and let me take a look at your car."

Handing him my keys, I followed him outside. So as to not get in the way, I stay on the porch while he pops the hood and starts poking around. He starts on one side and moves to the other, checking this or that, none of which I have any idea what they are.

The only things I know how to do under the hood of my vehicle is check the battery is hooked up, attach jumper cables if I need them, and refill windshield wiper fluid. Anything more than that and I am completely lost.

"Any idea what's wrong?" I ask after he's been looking at the engine for several minutes.

"Yeah, I have a pretty good idea. But I took the time to check over everything else. I might be able to get the parts here in

CHAPTER 4

Whiskey River. We'll have to see when we get into town," he says. Then he closes the hood and wipes his hand with a towel hanging out of his back pocket.

"Let's get going so we can get back before it gets dark," he says.

I follow him over to his truck where he opens the door for me and helps me inside before closing the door and going to his side.

The drive into Whiskey River is much like the drive to the cabin. It's long and windy, really, just a simple two-lane road. But the town itself is almost something you'd expect to see on TV. Well-manicured lawns and the buildings are all well maintained. The perfect Main Street USA for some TV show.

The town seems to sit in a valley with 360-degree views of mountains all over. This place has to be the best-kept secret in Montana. Today there seems to be some kind of festival going on. Main Street is blocked off, there are tents lining the road and people are everywhere. In order to get where we're going, we take a road behind all the shops.

We pull into Jack's shop and it is a lot bigger than what I was expecting in such a small town. In fact, it's easily the biggest shop on Main Street. When we walk in, there's a woman behind the counter. I would say maybe she's ten years older than me in her mid to late thirties.

"Jack! I didn't know you would be here today. Please tell me you're going to check out the brewery's grand opening," she says. Then she turns to me with a big smile and winks. "He really needs to get out and have some fun. Help me out here."

Right away, I like her and her bubbly personality.

"Maybe. How's everything going here, Katie?" Jack asks.

"Have a lot of good foot traffic with the grand opening today. I sold that bookcase that Phoenix brought in last week and they asked for two more just like it, so I have

CHAPTER 4

their information here for the next time he's in the shop."

"Phoenix is one of the other mountain men I told you about. Most of the furniture you see in here, he made by hand. His wife, Jenna, is the photographer." He points to the store walls where there are some of the most beautiful framed photos that I think I've ever seen.

"Katie, this is Sage. Could she sit here with you for a few minutes while I run to the back and send an e-mail to Phoenix and let him know about this order?"

"Oh, of course! I'll give her the official tour of the shop," Katie says, coming out from behind the counter and linking her arm in mine.

Jack smiles and goes to the back room.

"Yes, he's a nice guy," Katie says as we walk the perimeter of the shop.

"Oh, I didn't..." I start to say, but she stops me.

"You didn't have to ask the question. It's written all over your face. He is one of the best guys I've ever met, and I definitely know how easy it is to find the bad ones." Katie shakes her head.

"You and me both." I sigh.

"Are you from the women's shelter too, then?" she asks.

"No."

"I thought maybe you were. Jack here was a lawyer in his past life, and he does a lot of volunteer work at the women's shelter in Helena. Now the lawyer work he does is pro bono. Thankfully, he's kept his license active. That's how he and I met. Even though I know he didn't really need help here at the shop, I desperately needed a job to get on my feet, so he gave me one. Also, he's giving me a place to stay in the tiny studio space upstairs though, it's not really designed to be an apartment."

She goes on to point out different things around the shop and talks to me about who makes what, as if I have any clue who any of these people are. But she's nice and it's interesting to see what Jack is selling.

"Alright, are you ready to go before she fills your head with any more crazy stories? We can go check on the part for your car and then maybe spend a little time at the big event on Main Street. What do you say?" Jack asks as he emerges from the backroom.

Once again, I'm struck by how handsome he is, and he seems at ease here in the shop. So much so that I have to remind myself that he's just being nice, and this isn't a date.

Nice guys like him don't want damaged goods like me.

Chapter 5

Jack

Of course, they don't have the one car part that I really need to get her car going again. I guess I should be thanking the universe for small miracles. While we wait for the other part to get here, I am able to get a few smaller parts to do some tune ups on her car.

Even though I was willing to drive to Helena for the other part, they made some calls for me and it's not in stock there either. So waiting for it to get here is our only option at the moment. That's fine with me because it keeps her here longer and I can make sure that she is safe.

CHAPTER 5

Now I need to break the bad news to her. She's been waiting for me at the front of the store, staring out through the store's windows at all the fun and games of the grand opening while I've been dealing with the guy at the counter.

"So good news, bad news, and good news," I start with a smile, but I can see the worry in her eyes as soon as she turns around.

"Okay, the good news is they had almost everything that I needed to do some of the tune-ups that your car desperately needs. The bad news is they don't have the part in stock that I need to get your car up and running again, nor is it available in Helena. The other good news is they ordered it and it should be here next week. You are more than welcome to stay with me until then. In fact, I insist on it," I tell her. With each bit of information, I put it all out there and watch the emotion on her face.

"Are you sure I'm not in the way? I know the last thing you had planned on was sharing your cabin," she says, biting her bottom lip.

Reaching out, I use my thumb to tug her bottom lip from between her teeth. It's the first time we really touched each other, but it's just driving me crazy and I can't stand to watch her continue to do it and be expected to stay decent in public.

As she looks up at me when my skin touches hers for that brief moment, there's a look of pure wonder in her eyes. Even after I pull my thumb away, I can still feel her on it.

"I promise you're not in the way. Let's go check out this grand opening and show some hometown support, shall we?" I hold my hand out to her and she looks at it and for a moment I think she's not going to take it.

I don't know why I made the gesture. Even though I think it's mostly because of the crowd out there and I want to make sure she doesn't get lost in it, I still want to know that she is close by.

But instead of feeling relief when she takes my hand, an entirely different emotion fills my body. Mostly desire and lust. Holding her hand tight, I open the door and we step out into the crowd.

"This is the first brewery to open in Whiskey River," I tell her. "There have been talks of one a year or so ago, but instead they opened in a different town. We're all excited that they are now here. Hopefully, it'll bring in some more tourists for factory tours and for a taste of some local brew. Whiskey River is attempting to set itself up as the halfway point between Yellowstone National Park and Glacier National Park. It's perfect because of all the people that are traveling between the two locations every year. We want them to stop and spend time here in Whiskey River."

"Maybe it should have been a whiskey distillery as opposed to a brewery," she laughs, and the sound is absolutely beautiful.

"Not surprisingly, you are not the first person to suggest that," I laugh with her.

Pretty much every shop and business on Main Street is taking part. There are tents lining both sides of the road with art and craft vendors, along with chefs preparing different foods to try. It looks like people from the surrounding towns have come as well and turned it into a big event.

I let her lead the way. Whatever catches her eye, we stop and explore. There are many shops and booths we stop at and browse. I'm constantly scanning the area as if I have any clue what her ex looks like, but I still like to be aware of my surroundings.

"Jack!" Emelie calls out from a few booths over.

Instantly, Sage tenses up at the female voice, but right behind Emelie is her husband Axel. He's hard to miss because he's huge. Also, he's one of the first mountain men I met in the area.

"I'm so happy you decided to come and check out the grand opening! Oh, who's this?" Emelie asks when she sees Sage.

"This is Sage. She's friends with the guy I bought my cabin from," I say, keeping my explanation short and sweet.

Emelie is known for her matchmaking tendencies and I can already see the wheels in her head turning. She has set up many of Axel's other mountain man friends. Though I don't need her meddling with me, I doubt there's any way to stop her.

"Well hello, Sage. I'm Emelie and this is my husband, Axel. We live on the mountain, fairly close to Jack. The bakery has a fresh batch of their fudge. Why don't you come with me, and we'll go get some while we let the guys chat?" She loops her arm around Sage like they've been friends forever.

Sage looks back over at me, almost like she's asking if it's okay and if she can trust this girl.

"Go on ahead. I'll be there in just a few minutes. She can give you some of the details of the gossip around town," I tell Sage. As Sage and Emelie walk off talking, both Axel and I watch over them as they go to the bakery.

"So, how did you really meet her?" Axel asks once the girls are inside the building.

He's always been great at reading people and knowing when they're lying or not telling the whole truth.

"When I got home last night, she was in the cabin. Apparently, her college roommate is one of Greg's nieces and she had been told she could use the cabin anytime. Only she didn't know that the cabin had been sold. But when she went to leave last night, her car wouldn't start, so I let her stay the night. Today we came into town and the car parts that she needs have to be ordered so she'll be hanging around for a few days."

"You don't seem like that bothers you," he says, finally looking over at me.

"Can't say it does. There's something about that girl that draws me to her. I feel protective of her. She had a bruise on her arm where you could tell someone had grabbed her. Then she told me she was there thinking of what to do next after leaving her ex."

"Well, she's right up your alley then, isn't she?" Axel smirks.

CHAPTER 5

We cut through the crowd to the bakery where we join the girls who had grabbed the table in the back. After taking the two empty seats, we sit back and listen as Emelie is telling Sage about the people in town.

"You know Jack really is a good guy," Emelie says as she and Axel get ready to leave.

As we watch them leave, Sage says, "So nice to see the way her husband is with her."

"What the two of them have is really special. Watching them has made me realize I won't settle for anything less," I say, looking directly at Sage.

Not for the first time today, I'm picturing her as a person that could fill that role.

Chapter 6

Sage

On the way back to Jack's cabin, I relax and enjoy the scenery. It really is absolutely beautiful out here. Heading up the mountain, you go around a curve and there will be another beautiful view. Jack seems to know I enjoy them because he slows down for me to take them in.

"I can see why you like living up here. The drive alone is the most beautiful thing I've ever seen," I tell him.

"I thought that a time or two myself." He smiles, never taking his eyes off the road.

CHAPTER 6

The further we get from town, the more relaxed I become. Something about being in the crowd downtown set my anxiety on edge. It's like Mark could pop out of the crowd at any moment. Then trying to hide how I was feeling from Jack made it worse.

When I pictured heading into a small town like Whiskey River, I guess I imagined a few people on Main Street and maybe the brewery with a big 'Grand Opening' sign as people stopped in.

But it really was a festival where people from several towns in all directions came out. Though I got through it, and now have to convince myself I really am safe.

"Everything okay?" Jack asks as we pull into his driveway. It's over a mile long, leading up to his cabin, which gives a very secluded feel.

"Just thinking about everything. Still a lot to figure out." I give him part of the truth.

"Well, it doesn't have to all be figured out right now. Just try to relax a bit too. It's not good to make big decisions stressed out."

"Easier said than done."

With that, he chuckles and parks his truck beside the house.

"I know, sweetheart, it normally is."

The way he says sweetheart makes my cheeks heat and I don't hate it. As I follow him into the house, I find myself noticing different things than the last time I got here.

The house smells faintly of Jack and partly of pine, like the forest outside. There are some photos scattered around of what looks like him and his parents from different stages in their life.

The house is sparsely furnished, and I noticed there were a bunch of boxes in one of the spare bedrooms. I guess it's better to have them in there than staring at them all the time. Since we grabbed dinner while we were out, I'm not sure what we're going to do now.

While we ate, I talked a bit more to Katie, and Jack went over some of the books and stuff back at the shop. He said he wanted to make sure that Katie got to eat, but I get a feeling it was more than that. He likes knowing people around him are taken care of. I saw the same thing with the other mountain men he introduced me to and their wives. Thankfully, he seems to sense that I'm tired and jumps right into control.

"It's been a long day. Why don't you go take a nice leisurely bath and then get ready for bed? I think a good night's sleep will do you wonders."

"What about you?"

"I'm fine. There are some books here and I can read and relax." He points to the end table where he's got some books.

Of course, he's was right. The warm bath feels amazing. While he is getting ready for bed, I sneak into the kitchen for a snack. When he walks out in sweatpants and a long sleeve t-shirt, my mouth suddenly goes dry. The sweatpants hang low showing off that 'v' that points to interesting things as the t shirt rides up and molds to every muscle on his arms and chest.

"You should really try to get some sleep." He says gently before walking over to settle on the couch.

Going into the room alone doesn't appeal to me. Hell, I cut my bath short because I couldn't stand to be in the room alone. My anxiety today is making my mind race. Maybe I can stay out here with him until I get tired if I promise to be quiet.

"Actually, do you mind if I stay out here with you for a bit? I'm not tired and I don't really want to be alone."

He looks at me and studies me like he's attempting to figure me out. It's as if he's trying to determine what I'm not saying. Good luck to him on that because I don't even know what I'm not saying.

"You have to be tired. How about this? I'll take my book to the bedroom and lay down with you. That way, when you fall asleep, you're already in bed."

The thought of sharing a bed with him should make me tense and uneasy, but knowing that he'll be in the room with me actually calms me down. So, I nod and he picks up his book, and both he and Sadie head to the room. Jack's on the opposite side of the bed from where I'm at and Sadie lays down just inside the doorway.

When I lay down, I find myself slightly relaxing. But then knowing that there's someone sitting beside me, and he's wide awake, makes it harder for me to fall asleep. I look over at him and it's like he can sense that I'm watching him.

"Go to sleep," he whispers.

"I don't know if I can with you lying in bed like this."

"Is it the light that's bothering you?" he asks, setting his book down and looking over at me.

"I don't know. Possibly?"

He nods and marks his place in his book before setting it on the nightstand and reaching over to turn off the light. He then settles in and lies down on the bed, on top of the covers.

"You didn't have to do that," I tell him, realizing I've now disrupted his whole evening plan of reading.

He had left the light on in the living room, which gives enough light through the doorway that I can see he's laying down facing me just like I'm facing him. As we stare at each other for a moment, I try to figure out what to say to fill the silence.

The tension in the air is thick, but it's not bad tension. It doesn't make me uncomfortable. We continue to stare at each other and I try to memorize the details of his face because I know when I'm gone, I'll be thinking of moments just like this.

How gentle his eyes look, the small scar at his hairline on his forehead, his dark chocolate brown eyes, and his full lips. Those lips I can't stop staring at and wondering what they would feel like on mine. When I look back up at his eyes, a sizzling heat is in them. Then he runs his hand through my hair and rests it on the back of my head.

He lowers his face to mine, hesitating for only a moment before he kisses me. His lips are softer than I thought they would be, and when he pulls me closer to him, I can't get close enough. I wrap my arms around his neck, and like our bodies are magnets, we are drawn to each other until there is no space between us.

His kisses are gentle. I'm happy he's taking his time to explore me. I can tell he's as turned on as I am by his hard length pressing into me and I don't ever want this kiss to end. This amazing feeling of pure bliss is my new addiction.

He rolls me over on my back and braces himself on top as he keeps kissing me. He then uses one hand to explore my body, over my breasts, but once he moves toward my stomach, I tense.

"Hey, what happened just now?" He pulls back to look me in the eyes.

I wasn't always a thick girl, but in college from the stress I started to gain some curves and I've always been self-conscious about it. It didn't help that Mark constantly pointed them out and suggested I stop eating to lose weight.

"Well, I'm not a skinny girl. I mean, I used to be, but somewhere along the line I gained weight that I just can't seem to shake..."

"Sweetheart, I've seen your curves and they are a huge part of what has been turning me on all day."

"Mark always told me I needed to lose weight. That it... um, it wasn't a turn-on." I can feel the heat on my face as I admit that to Jack.

I know this whole conversation all together is probably the biggest turn off.

"I'm sorry. This is probably not very sexy. I've always been awkward like that." I moan, throwing my head back against the pillow and closing my eyes.

Jack doesn't respond or move until I open my eyes.

"I want you to listen to me and listen to me good. Okay?" He pauses and I nod.

CHAPTER 6

"I love your curves. You better not lose any weight. In fact, I'd be okay if you put on a few more pounds. I am going to need something to hold on to when I fuck you so hard with how damn turned on I will be around you all the time. As for being awkward? It's absolutely fucking adorable. Now, all that being said, I won't force you into anything you don't want. But I can assure you I want you." He presses his hard cock into my thigh.

"I want you too," I whisper because I'm afraid this is all a dream, and any loud noises will jolt me awake.

"Yeah?" He asks, searching my eyes and again I just nod.

A sexy smile crosses his face as he leans in and kisses me again. When his hands run under my shirt, I tense just a little but he moves slowly and takes his time. A move that makes me even hotter and teases me all at the same time.

He explores every inch of me as he slowly removes his clothes and mine until we are both naked in bed. Without taking his eyes off me, he reaches for the condom. Slightly self-conscious again, I try to pull the blanket over me.

"Don't hide from me. I'll make you walk around this cabin naked at all times until you understand how beautiful you truly are. Just the way you are," he says rolling the condom on and climbing back into bed.

"I'm sorry," I say. Then I focus on him and not on how naked I am in front of him.

Having his eyes roam over me is almost too much. It's as if he's running his hand over me. Every place his eyes touch, tingles and they travel straight to my core.

He climbs between my legs and slowly spreads them wide. Everything with this man is done slowly and with intention. I fight every instinct to slam my legs shut and not let myself be vulnerable to him.

"Already so wet for me. I love it." He runs a finger over my pussy.

Then he leans in and smoothed his tongue over my slit and my hips jerk from the blissful sensation.

Wrappings his arms around my thighs to hold me in place, he takes his time feasting on me. There is no other way to describe it. This isn't just for my enjoyment, even though I thoroughly love every minute of his exploration. But this is for his enjoyment too, and he's taking his time savoring me.

I try to move and angle my hips to get the pressure where I need it but the more I move, the tighter he holds me down until he turns and bites the side of my thigh.

"Stop moving or I drag this out even longer," he growls and goes back in for another taste.

I fight the need to move and end this delicious torture, he sucks on my clit, hard, and I explode in a million sensations. The next thing I know, he's on top of me and sliding into me while the tremors still rock my body.

"Fuck, you feel good squeezing my dick like that," he groans.

As I start to relax, he slides all the way into me and we both groan. I feel so full, almost too full, but being connected to Jack like this is the most intimate feeling I've ever experienced.

The way he's looking in my eyes proves this is more than just sex. This is us connecting on a whole new level. Down to our souls. His eyes stay on mine as he slowly starts sliding in and out of me. I run my hands through his hair and down his neck.

Then he moves his hips and hits a spot inside of me that sets my whole body on fire. My nails dig into his back, which seems to set him off even more. Before I know it, I'm cumming again.

"Scream for me. I love how vocal you are." He whispers in my ear.

I hadn't even realized I was screaming, but I throw my head back as another orgasm hits me. Then I hear his groans and feel his cock pulse inside of me.

We both lay there for a moment before he goes to the bathroom and cleans up. He then gets in bed and pulls me into his arms and holds me tight before pulling the covers over me.

"Tell me about this bruise." He gently traces the one on my arm he saw yesterday.

"I was trying to leave, and he wasn't happy. So I agreed to stay and then packed up and left when he was in to work the next morning," I tell him. At the same time, trying not to let myself relive the moment.

"And this one?" He traces my shoulder blade.

"He was drunk and mad at me for eating dinner without him. It was after ten at night by this point. He pushed me and I fell against the coffee table, and he told me that I deserved it."

"You know you didn't. He deserves it." He says, kissing my neck.

"I hear people say it, but I don't know. I saw my mom in these kinds of relationships and when she'd reach out for help, she wouldn't get it. She'd feared for her life, so she learned to just take it. It at least put a roof over her head and food on the table for me."

He's quiet for a moment before answering and his voice is level, like he's trying to control it.

"Well, I'm not letting that happen to you. Stay here with me. Anything you want to do, I will make sure it happens. You are safe here. There is no reason to go back," he says.

I want to believe him because for the first time in my whole life, I do feel safe.

"What about you? Why are you up here all alone? A lawyer who gave up high-profile cases?" I ask him to shift the conversation.

"Those high-profile cases are good for money but not good for the soul. I have plenty of money, but knowing I defended criminals and got people off that should have been in jail doesn't sit well with me to this day."

"Well, you didn't know…"

"No, I knew. They would look me in the eyes, and admit they did it, but I was told I had to defend them to keep my job. I did that for longer than I should have." He sounds disgusted with himself.

"So now you do pro bono work for women like Katie, who really need it. All the while thinking doing enough good will cancel out the bad," I fill in what he isn't saying.

He doesn't agree with me, but he doesn't deny it either.

"It's working because it brought me you." He holds me tighter and I can't remember the last time I felt as wanted as I do right here in his arms.

This could be my future. Falling asleep each night in Jack's arms, feeling safe and wanted.

It's so easy to let myself believe and forget the fact that girls like me don't end up with guys like Jack.

Chapter 7

Jack

Today, I've decided Sage needs a lesson on how to be alone. I don't want her to ever feel like she has to jump into another relationship because she doesn't want to be alone. Of course, I'm hoping that she will want something with me, but I want that to be a choice, not a necessity.

"I'm glad you at least thought to bring some decent shoes coming into the mountains and all," I tell Sage when I see her step out of the bedroom after I told her to go get ready for a hike.

CHAPTER 7   59

She has decent walking shoes, jeans, and a few layered tops. It's not perfect, but it will do for what I have in mind.

"Come on, I want to take you to the entire reason that I bought this land." Taking her hand. I lead her out the back door with Sadie hot on our heels.

"You mean you didn't buy the property for the awesome cabin that needs a ton of work?" She sasses me and I stop to turn around to look at her because it was the first time I'd heard her personality emerge.

Her face instantly falls.

"I'm sorry. I didn't mean..."

"Don't apologize. It's just the first time you've had a little bit of sass in you, and I like it," I tell her. Then I adjust my growing hard on because of all the images that popped into my head of what I want to do with her sassy mouth.

The most beautiful shade of pink tints her cheeks, but she smiles, and that's all I ever want is her happiness and safety.

We continue walking with Sadie leading the way. I haven't owned this property for long, but we've already made quite a few trips out here. If I had my guess, I'd say Sadie's been out here a few times on her own as well.

Along the way, I point out different things to her. Berry bushes, trees, and plants and what they can be used for that sort of thing. We walk along the river for a while, which prompts me to share how Emelie and Axel met.

"This river travels through much of the mountainside. If you were to head upriver, you would be able to pass pretty close by Axel's cabin. That's how Axel and Emelie met in the river." I smile because I absolutely love their story.

"Like actually in the river? I would assume out here in the mountains it would be freezing cold!"

"Well, just like down in Yellowstone National Park, we have a few hot springs in the area that feeds in the river and keep it pretty warm spring through fall. And yes, actually in the river. Axel was bathing in the river and Emelie had gotten lost and stumbled across him. She had been camping with her ex when she caught him cheating and he left her in the woods by herself. Axel says it was almost nightfall and with the storm rolling in, he didn't have a choice but to offer her a place to stay. Then the roads washed out and by the time the roads were clear, she had made it known she wasn't leaving and the rest is history."

"That is so cute and I can definitely picture it with the two of them. It was meant to be, and the universe stepped in big time." She sighs with a smile on her face as she looks out over the river.

"You know I never really thought about it that way, but yeah, I can definitely see it," I tell her as we continue walking.

The hike starts to head uphill and we stop a few times to let her catch her breath. She definitely isn't used to a more strenuous hike. But to be honest, I could use a few breaks myself.

"Wow," she says in awe once we reach the top of the trail and everything opens up.

"Come on, the best part is right over here, so watch your step." I grab her hand and lead her over to the edge.

There's a large rock that juts out the side of the mountain. This cliff is the most peaceful place I've ever found in my life. Then I sit down on the edge with my feet dangling over.

"Come sit with me." I pat the spot next to me and she slowly moves but crosses her legs, not setting them over the edge as I did.

"It's beautiful up here," she says, taking in the view. You can see for miles down the river, and in the valley between this mountain. It's absolutely stunning because you can see over the treetops from here.

Not only is this place a great place for hunting along the river, but mostly it's the place I come to when I need to think.

"Now close your eyes and just listen," I tell her. But it takes her a moment before she does.

I don't make a sound. I simply sit and watch her until a few seconds later her eyes open again.

"I hear nothing."

"Exactly. Now close your eyes and just be in the moment of nothing."

We do this exercise a few times before I can see the peace and serenity finally flow over her. Eventually, she lies down on the ground and I lay down next to her enjoying the beautiful day and the quiet.

I keep waiting for her to ask to leave or head back home or even to talk. But she surprises me most of all when an hour passes and we're still enjoying the silence together.

"You ready to go back down to the cabin?" I finally ask, sitting up.

"Do you plan to hunt around here?" she asks and just like that, we're talking about my plans and how I'd like to live off the land

and she's asking genuine questions making me think she might actually be interested.

My mind starts to wonder about what it would be like to have a life with her out here. She could manage the garden while I worked in the shop and hunted. Maybe she'd start quilting like Emelie and the other wives do. Those quilts sell quickly in the shop and I can't keep them in stock.

Regardless of what her choice would be, I know I want her here with me and I will do whatever I can to make that happen.

Her walking away is no longer an option.

Chapter 8

Sage

We got to the shop early just as Katie was getting ready to open.

"I knew you'd be here for the meeting today," Katie greets us as we come in and she starts flipping on the lights.

"I haven't missed one of these meetings and I don't plan to start now," Jack says as he turns on his computer in the back.

"The mountain men meet once a month, sometimes twice to bring things in, pick up what they have Jack order for them. That sort of thing. The group started as four guys, but as they got married it grew, and they have been adding some friends to the group as well." Katie says as I walk with her.

After she turns all the lights on, she sets up the cash register and checks the voicemail before unlocking the door and turning on the 'we are open' lights.

She goes on talking about how the weekend went at the shop and I keep glancing through the back door to where Jack is sitting at his desk working. It is like he can sense my eyes on him and looks up.

At that moment when our eyes meet, I feel like a real-life version of the emoji with the hearts for eyes. When he smiles, it's as if we're the only two of us on Earth. The trance is broken when Katie calls my name to get my attention.

As things begin to get busy, I let Katie work and move to the back room with Jack. Pulling out my phone, I start reading a book when my phone rings, I freeze.

"Who is it?" Jack asks when I don't answer.

"It's Mark, my ex," I deny the call, and still a little shaken, I put the phone down.

"Hey, come here," he says, holding his hand out to me. When I take it, he pulls me onto his lap.

"You have me, and he won't hurt you again, okay? Is there any reason you need to see him again?" Jack asks.

"No, I mean I left some clothes there, but they can be replaced. Anything else I wanted, I kept in my car."

"Good. So just put it out of your mind and have some fun with the girls. I know you will enjoy meeting them."

Almost like he summoned them, in walks Axel and Emelie followed by Bennett and Willow, who I met the other day.

"I'm so excited you are here!" Emelie says, running over to give me a hug.

She then loops her arm through mine, pulling me back out into the shop where Katie is. All the while talking about how she can't wait for me to meet Jana, Jenna, and Hope.

Emelie, Willow, and Katie all start talking about people in town and what's going on and they take the time to explain who is who and what they are talking about, trying their best to include me.

When the other women walk in, another round of introductions happens as the guys slowly start to trickle in after unloading their stuff in the back room.

The guys gravitate to their wives' sides, and I notice each one of them is somehow touching their girl. It's either a hand on their waist, an arm wrapped around their shoulder, or they're just holding hands. When Jack joins them standing behind me, resting his hands on my hips, and kissing the top of my head, I almost melt.

Is this what it's like to be in a healthy friend circle? I've never had friends like this before or even been included in Mark's circle of friends. This has been so easy. Hell, I'm starting to realize I don't think I've ever had a healthy relationship, so everything that happens feels different, but in a good way.

"So, while you guys do your thing, the girls and I want to head down to the café and get some coffee and a snack and chit-chat about you boys. We will stick together and be back in a bit," Emelie says.

All the guys glance at each other before looking at their girls and it's a sight to watch. Kisses are exchanged and every one of the guys tells their girl to be careful and stick together.

"Hey, this means you, too. Stick with them and be cautious," Jack whispers in my ear before turning me to face him.

He kisses me in front of everyone and I almost moan out loud. I've never had anyone want to kiss me in front of people. Not quite knowing what to do because I'm so used to the no PDA speech, I don't move.

"Go be safe," he says with a smile, but I see a look of concern there, too.

"I will I promise," I say, kissing his cheek.

He slips something into my hand and when I look down, I find money there.

"Jack..." I whisper.

"Just go have fun with the girls. You can yell at me later." He says with a cocky grin that tells me I won't win this one. Instead, I nod and follow the girls out the door.

Looking back one more time, not only do I find all the men staring after their girls, but Jack's eyes are on me and it makes me feel safe and wanted.

Strange feelings for a girl like me. The mixed emotions of what I'm used to and what I am feeling are setting me a little off balance but in the best possible way.

The girls and I walk down the street to the bakery the next block over, and go in, placing our orders. I get a coffee and a muffin.

As we pick up our treats, we claim a table by the window and start talking.

"So, what brings you to Whiskey River?" Hope asks.

"Oh, had an... incident with my ex-boyfriend and needed a place to clear my mind. So I came to stay at my college roommate's uncle's place that I was told I could use whenever. My roommate and I came out here a few times to study because it was quiet and peaceful. Well, I didn't know Jack had bought it, so we met that night and then my car broke down so I've been stuck here." I laugh it off.

"It seems more like Jack is planning to keep you here," Willow says as she walks up and sits down. "Emelie will be a few minutes as she ordered some fancy drink they are making," she laughs.

"As much as she loves it out here, I think she misses some of the big city conveniences the most," Jenna says and the girls all agree.

When the bell over the door rings, I look up and freeze.

"What's wrong? Do you know that man?" Jana, who is sitting next to me, whispers in my ear.

"That is my ex, Mark!" I start to panic. There is no way to get around him, get out the door and there's no way to go out another way.

"There you are. I don't like this game of hide and seek," Mark says loud enough the entire shop stops to look at him.

Emelie, who hasn't sat down yet, doesn't say anything but her face screams who is this? My only hope is she realizes I need help, and will leave to get the guys.

"Mark, we broke up. What are you doing here?" I say loud enough for her to hear.

I don't look at Emelie, because I don't want to draw Mark's attention to her. But via my peripheral vision, I can see that she gets the point and whispers to the person across the counter. Then carefully, without drawing any attention, walks behind Mark and out the door.

"I'm here to bring you home. You had your little adventure. Now it's time to stop playing games," he says. Then he takes a step toward me.

I just have to keep him calm until Jack and the other men can get here. I know they will help me.

I have support now. I know it with every fiber of my being.

CHAPTER 9

JACK

I'm at the shop talking to the guys about the different sales trends that I'm seeing. We are also talking about the big hunt that the guys do every summer, the one that I'm invited to this year now that I officially live up on the mountain.

When the bell goes off indicating someone's coming through the door, I'm praying it's the girls because I'm ready for them to be back, even though they just left. All the guy's eyes go to the door and when I turn around and only see Emelie walking in the door. I know something is wrong.

CHAPTER 9

"Little One..." Axel starts, probably to criticize her for not staying with the other girls. But she holds up her hand and looks directly at me and my heart sinks.

"We were getting out orders and sitting down to talk when a guy walked in. I was still at the counter so he didn't realize I was part of the group, but it sounded like it was Sage's ex, Mark," she says.

I don't think I've ever moved so fast in my life, but I know the other men are right behind me.

"I'll stay here with Emelie and Katie. When the other girls are safe, send them in," Axel says. I'm sure he's not willing to leave his wife with the chance of danger lurking.

I also know that it's killing him to not come and help, but it's the mountain men's code that we protect our girls first, always. The guys up here aren't strangers to kidnappings and worse. There's a reason most of us move to the mountains, to get away from people.

I'm one store down from the bakery when a man walks out, gripping Sage by her arm.

"Mark, calm down. We can talk with out making a scene," she says and even though I can tell she's trying to keep her voice calm, she is anything but.

"I'm going in with the girls," Cash says.

I can't fault them for wanting to make sure their girls are safe. I know I'd be in the same situation. That leaves me with Phoenix, Bennett, and Cole. That's plenty of muscle if I need it. Plus, we are only two blocks away from the police station and I'm sure Cash is calling them now because I can see him on his phone through the huge picture window.

"I suggest you get your hands off of her," I say, walking up to Mark and Sage.

That's when Mark turns around, and I can see his face clearly for the first time. I feel like I've been sucker punched. I know this man. I defended this man in my old life for nearly beating his girlfriend to death after raping her and then he left her for dead.

Thankfully, someone found her, and she lived.

This was the case that put me over the edge and made me quit and move out here to Whiskey River. I knew Mark was guilty. He pretty much bragged about how gullible his parents were and how their money could get him out of anything. Their money was paying his legal fees because he had them convinced this girl was making it up to get their money.

Now here he is doing the same thing. Only my Sage was smart enough to get away early and he wasn't going to have it. If she goes back with him, she is as good as dead. I know men like him.

The worst part is the fact that she is going through all of this because of me. How will she ever forgive me? Because I sure as hell won't be able to forgive myself. But I will make sure she is safe and will stop this asshole once and for all.

Thankfully, in my moment of panic and dread, the other guys stepped up and Cole has Mark pinned to the ground. I was right about Cash calling the cops because our buddy Detective Greer shows up with several uniformed cops and takes over.

While Bennett and his wife, Willow, take care of Sage, I switch into lawyer mode. I'm going to make sure Mark is locked away for a good long time. I owe Sage at least that. Hell, if I could, I would have thrown him off the cliff, so she would never have to worry about him again. Only then I'd be the one behind bars, but for my Sage, it would be worth it.

We all watch the cops carry him off to jail. With the three guys there they make him walk the two blocks to the police station. I'm pretty sure the whole town was watching.

When I finally turn back to Sage she runs into my arms and holds me tight, but not a word is said.

"Let's get back to the shop and away from prying eyes," Bennett says. Everyone has their eyes on us and they don't even try to hide it.

Nodding, I wrap my arm around Sage and lead her back to the shop. Willow relayed everything to Emelie, Katie, and Axel, who I'm sure were watching through the shop windows.

"Are you okay?" Sage asks me when everyone quiets down.

"You need to go stay with Emelie and Axel. They will keep you safe and make sure you have what you need to get back on your feet." I tell her and the whole shop goes deadly quiet.

"What? Why?" Sage asks, panic in her voice.

"Because I'm the reason he's able to hurt you."

"You know that's not true, man," Cole says. But I shake my head. "Mark's case was the last case I defended before I left my job and moved out here. He nearly beat a girl to death, raped her, and left her for dead. Thankfully, she survived but his parents have money and because they had so much of it, they were willing to use it. I was forced to defend him. He admitted and bragged about what he did and how he wouldn't be charged with it. The day he walked away scot free, I saw the broken look on that girl's face and I was done. I walked away and I haven't been the same since."

"So, you have been doing pro bono work for the women's shelter and giving people like me a job when you don't really need help. I also see the books, Jack. I know you send a woman named Lisa money every month. I'm guessing that's her?" Katie says and I just nod.

"Money is a poor excuse of a way to make things right, but it's the only thing I could do. To make sure she was able to get the help she needs. With my help, she was able to go back to school and is now a lawyer fighting for the good guys." While I am so proud of her, at the same time she never should have been in that situation and it's my entire fault.

"Mark, hurting me isn't your mistake, Jack," Sage says and tries to place a hand on my chest, but I move out of her reach. "I made the choice to ignore the red flags, and I made the choice to be with him. If I hadn't, I wouldn't have been here and met you."

Shaking my head, I look over at Axel.

"Will you take her back to your place and help her out?" I ask him, ignoring her pleas.

"Of course. We will make sure she is safe," he says as Emelie walks over to Sage and wraps her in a hug.

I don't look at anyone else. Turning away, I walk out the door and head home. When I park my truck, I don't even go inside. I just call for Sadie, grab a bottle of water from my truck, and go straight to the cliff.

What are the fucking odds Sage's ex was the last client I defended? The one with the most brutal case? The one that still haunts me at night.

How can she ever forgive me for what I've done? I know once she gets to Axel and

Emelie's place and processes everything. She will be just as disgusted with me as I am with myself.

Lying down, I let the sun warm me and try to ignore the images of the last time I was here.

With her.

Chapter 10

Sage

Walking into Axel and Emelie's house, I collapse right on the couch. I try to focus on the details, the stone fireplace, the large room, and the books. Focusing on the details I am hoping will keep me from thinking of Jack and what just happened.

I'm on overload between Mark showing up and the bomb Jack dropped on us and then him walking away. I think the slightest breeze could have carried me away, making me wonder if this is what shock feels like.

"Why don't you make us some hot chocolate, My Giant? I think she needs something comforting," Emelie asks. Then she sits down on the couch beside me and pulls me in for a hug. Axel wraps a blanket around us, starts the fire in the fireplace, and then goes to the kitchen to do as his wife asked.

"I know it hurts right now, but I think you should stay here for a few days. Clear your head, and allow the car parts to get here. Then Axel will handle getting your car and your stuff, okay?" she says.

Her voice is so soft, and it seems like she already has a plan in place, so it's hard to say no. At this point, I'm willing to let her and Axel take the lead because I don't even want to think about this crappy day anymore.

In what seems like the blink of an eye, Axel is in front of me, holding out a cup of hot chocolate. I take it and he offers the other one to his wife before going to the kitchen to grab his own.

"For as long as I've known Jack, he was been trying to make up for something in his past. He was always doing for others much more than most people would. It took me a while to learn why. Those days at the law firm really haunt him and I can't imagine what it's like for him to come face to face with that today," Axel says.

"I can't even imagine. I'm sure he just needs some time to process." Emelie says as we drink the hot chocolate. "You know that I don't think any of us couples on the mountain had an easy start."

Axel chuckles and nods his head in agreement.

"Take us, for example. I was camping with my ex-boyfriend..." She starts and stops when Axel actually growls at the mention of her ex.

"Oh hush," Emelie giggles. "Anyway, we were camping, and I found out he was cheating on me so I went for a walk to cool down. I came back to the campsite, and he was gone, and all of our stuff was gone. Panicking, I took off thinking I'd catch up with him in the parking lot, only I ended up going the wrong way and stumbled upon Axel bathing naked in the river."

"Thankfully, you have gotten much better at telling directions," he chuckles and shakes his head. The smile on his face makes it clear as day the love he has for her.

"I had no choice but to trust him. Not only was I miles from town, with no idea how to get there, but there was a storm rolling in, and the sun was setting. So, we came back here, got stranded by the road washing out and I never left. That makes it sound all easy and fun, right?" she says.

I wonder at her point, so I play along. "Yeah, it does."

"What I don't tell in that story is that when the roads opened, we ended up at the police station answering questions for hours until Jack stepped in all because my ex accused Axle of kidnapping me. Then we had to go into Billings to get all my stuff and came face to face with the girl my ex had been cheating on me with who was staying in our apartment while we were gone. You don't hear about me pushing aside my fear of going from one guy to another. Or the fact that the whole first year Axel was on pins and needles waiting for me to leave, thinking I didn't want a life up here on the mountain. Hell, look at Hope and Cash, she and Jana were kidnapped. It brought Jana to Cole, but they had to deal with that trauma. Though none of the rest of us can top a kidnapping," Emelie laughs.

"I see your point."

I don't hear much of what is said after that as I zone out. The next thing I know, I'm being shown to a guest room.

"Here on the dresser are towels and such. You look about my size and in the dresser are a bunch of my work clothes. Feel free to wear whatever fits. The bathroom is the next room over to the left. Extra blankets are in the closet. Our room is at the end of the hall if you need us. You know where the kitchen is. Help yourself to anything, any time. No need to ask. There are a bunch of romance books in the bin under the bed, so read whatever you want," Emelie says. Then she hugs me one more time before turning around and going out the door.

The bedroom is nice, with typical log cabin walls and a window above the queen-size bed. On one wall is the closet door that I open to grab an extra blanket. Peering inside, I can see the closet also stores winter coats and hunting camo.

The other side of the room has shelving units along the wall filled with a mix of items, including some canned food. Also, there are some items for Emelie's crafts that she sells at Jack's store, and some other miscellaneous items.

It's smart of them to use all the extra space in the cabin. They truly live off the land and try not to leave the house as much as possible. I love this way of life. I have never felt more relaxed than being here on the mountain. The last few days, I was starting to think I might never have to leave. But now I have no idea what I'm going to do.

Getting ready for bed, I turn off the lights and lie in the darkness. I notice how quiet it is out here in the middle of nowhere. If I got up to look out the window, maybe I'd see different animals roaming around. Right now, even at night with the moon shining bright in the sky, it gives me just enough light to see around the room to remind me that I'm not in my own space. In a way, it's comforting to know that I don't have to fall into old patterns and old habits and that tomorrow isn't just a routine day. But at the same time, it's scary too.

As I play over in my head the events that happened today, I think about what Emelie said earlier tonight. Then I make a decision. Tomorrow morning I'm going to go talk to Jack. He doesn't get to just make a decision concerning the both of us. We have a right to discuss this together. At least after everything, I think I deserve that consideration. If it doesn't work out after we talk, so be it. Then I'll take Axel up on his offer to get my stuff and we can leave Jack in peace.

Chapter 11

Jack

Falling asleep outside on top of a cliff and waking up to your dog licking your face, thinking that you might be dead is a hell of a way to wake up. I stayed up on that cliff so long that I actually fell asleep and thinking back, I don't recommend it. Even though I must have been so tired that I didn't move, thankfully I didn't roll off and fall down the mountain. I might have woken up at the bottom of the mountain if I had woken up at all.

The early morning walk in the fresh air back to the cabin really seems to help clear my mind. All the good that I've been doing would be for nothing if I didn't take this chance to make things right. This is the ultimate chance to fix the one wrong that has been haunting me.

So, before I even take a shower, my first phone call is to the police station to talk to Detective Greer. Since this man is single and dedicated to his work, I know he'll be there at this early hour, especially with a case like Mark's.

And of course, he picks up when I call. We spent about an hour going over everything that I know about him. After investigating Mark, Greer was able to learn that I defended him and he can't be recharged for that crime. But that was quite a few years ago, so the chances that he wasn't with anyone until Sage was very slim. Now we need to look for and track previous cases where women have come forward and show a history.

My next call is to Lisa. The woman who I sat across from in court for weeks as she had to face her rapist and watch me discredit her at every turn, even when I knew Mark was guilty.

We've only talked a handful of times in the last few years. But she does deposit my check every month. The first time we talked, she told me to stop sending them. I broke down on the phone and cried. I apologized and told her that I would never forgive myself.

Then I begged her to take those checks. If she didn't want them for herself, to at least go out and do some good with them. She agreed and I don't know what she does with the checks, but she deposits them. Every time I feel like it's a tiny crumble, a piece of dust falling off the huge rock of this horrible thing that I did.

"Jack?" She answers the phone all confused, and I can't blame her. What reason could she possibly think of that I would be calling her?

After I tell her everything, I'm convinced that he's doing this again. Knowing without a doubt in my gut that there have to have been other girls in between. I felt immense relief and it radiated through the phone when I told her that he was currently in custody and would be staying there for at least the next week. I even go on to tell her how I walked away from Sage. I hold nothing back.

"I want to be there, Jack. I want to be in the courtroom, and I want to see if he can wiggle his way out of it this time." Lisa says with so much determination there's no way I could say no.

"That's your choice. Just make sure you're really thinking this through. This does mean facing him."

"I know and at the very least, maybe having me there will rattle him and make him slip up. At least we can hope. I wish I could do something more to help. The best I can do is ask around and see if anyone knows who he's been with or can give us an idea of who to talk to. Even finding one other person could drastically help the case, right?" She sounds so hopeful.

"It absolutely could. Any lead you could find would be a huge help."

"Good, then it looks like I will be seeing you soon. We can make a difference this time. Jack, I feel it," she says before hanging up.

I wish I felt as confident as she did. Now for the biggest part and the one person that we absolutely need for this case. I won't let Lisa down again because letting Lisa down again means letting Sage down and that just isn't an option. I'll play dirty if I have to. Whatever it takes.

Because failing this time just isn't an option.

Next, I go into town to do the one thing that I could think of to help Sage and I hope it will be enough for now. I know there's absolutely no way she'll want me back after all this, but at the very least, I can keep her close and make sure she stays safe.

I rent her an apartment in town, one that has an excellent security system and is right across the street from the grocery store and bakery, right down the block from the police station. It's probably the safest apartment you could ask for in Whiskey River.

Even so, I change out the locks and add a few extra security measures before going back up the mountain to Emelie and Axel's place where Sage is staying for now.

I knock on the door then take a step back. I know that Axel's going to be answering the door with a shotgun. Though I'm sure he's probably expecting me after everything yesterday.

Sure enough, he opens the door, shotgun in hand, but drops it when he sees me. The expression on his face says it all. Have I come here to fix what I screwed up or am I going to cause more problems? I shrug because I honestly don't know.

For a moment I think he's not even going to let me in the door, but then he steps back, and I go inside to find Emelie and Sage sitting on the couch. Sage's eyes go wide when she sees me and Emelie looks over at her for just a moment before standing up. Without a word, she takes Axel's hand and leads them to the back of the room to the kitchen counter.

They're looking out for Sage, and as much as I would love a bit of privacy with her, I'm thankful for it as well. I know she's in good hands with them.

"I talked with Detective Greer this morning and Mark is behind bars and will be for several days. I'm hoping you'll press charges and give me another chance to put him behind bars where he deserves. Not only for you but to allow me to make things right with Lisa."

"The woman from the trial you told me about?" she asks hesitantly and I just nod.

She looks back over at Emelie and Axel, but I can't take my eyes off her. She just looks so beautiful. Being out here on the mountain agrees with her. More than I ever thought possible.

"You're going to need to stay in the area, so I rented you an apartment in town. It has a security system and brand new locks, and multiple security measures. Plus, it's right on Main Street and you can see the police station from there, so it's one of the safest places to stay in town. There's an animal shelter that's about thirty minutes away with several dogs that will make great guard dogs as another layer of security."

As I tell her about the apartment, she gets a funny look on her face and I wonder if she didn't have plans to stay or if she doesn't have plans to press charges and I'm putting the cart before the horse.

"Please tell me you at least plan to press charges?" I ask, needing to make sure.

"Well, of course I'm going to press charges. Seeing how much this means to you, there was never an option not to. But I don't want to live in town," she says.

At her words, my heart sinks. Of course, she hadn't planned to stick around, and I can't blame her. But if she's not here, it's just so much harder to watch over her and make sure that she's okay.

"I understand. But just to make sure that wherever you end up, I know how to get ahold of you. There's going to be a lot to do for this case and stuff that we're going to need to go over. Lisa is trying to help me find any other women that Mark would have done this to between his time with her and his time with you. All we need is one more to show a pattern."

"I never knew he dated anyone named Lisa, but he was dating a girl named Julie before me. When they broke up, she switched schools. I never thought too much about it. I thought they broke up because she was going to a different school. And it's not that I don't want to live in town, it's just that I would rather live on the mountain with you."

I freeze because there's no way I heard what I just heard, even after everything she's not wanting to run away screaming.

"Sage..." I start, but she holds her hand up and I stop talking, waiting to hear what she had to say.

"What happened with Mark and me was not your fault. I don't blame you for it and you've got to stop blaming yourself. The justice system doesn't always work, and it's always favored those who have money. That's why men like you have to work hard for women like Lisa and Katie. The fact that you stepped away from all the money and from what essentially was your dream to do what was right says what an amazing guy you are and you can't convince me otherwise."

Every word she says tugs at my heart. How does this woman see me so differently than I even see myself?

"I love you, Sage. If you can look past all of this and you still want to be with me, that would be the most amazing gift in the world. If you can't, I understand as well."

"I love you too. And of course, I see the good in you. It's always easier to see the bad in ourselves than the good that everyone else sees." She smiles and then lunges at me so fast that I barely have time to catch her.

But I do.

Having her back in my arms is the most freeing feeling I've ever felt. I hold her tight, so tight, because there's no way I want to let go. When she looks up at me, there's nothing but pure love and happiness in her eyes. I don't ever want to do anything to take that away.

Leaning in, I give her a soft gentle kiss because I'm still aware of our audience. The moment her lips touch mine though, I feel like I'm home again.

"Hey Jack?" she whispers against my lips.

"Yeah?" I ask but try to lean in for another kiss, which causes her to giggle.

"Take me to the cliff," she says with a mischievous glint in her eye. There's no way I'm telling her no.

"Let's go home."

Epilogue

Sage

A few months later...

It's funny how much your life can change in just a few short months. I was supposed to just be in Whiskey River for a few days at most. Instead, it turns out this is where I was meant to be. These are my people and this is where I feel at home.

With Jack's help and blessing, I decided to finish my degree online. Though I'm taking it slowly and only going to school part-time, but planning to take extra classes in the winter when we are stuck inside more. That way it will leave summer free because we are learning together how to homestead and live off the land.

Of course, we have the help of Axel and the other guys, but it is still a big learning curve for both of us. Jack has done a lot of research over the last few years, but learning it from a book and actually doing it are two completely different things.

Mark is still sitting behind bars because his parents have cut him off completely. The first time he was charged with assault and domestic abuse it was easy to believe that she was making it up for the money. But the second time was a bit harder to swallow. When we filed our claims that we wanted no money just justice I think it pushed them over the edge to realize that we weren't after him for his family's money.

A couple of weeks ago, I received a phone call from his parents apologizing for enabling their son to continue this behavior. They then offered to pay for a lawyer if I couldn't afford it. I thanked them for it but declined because I have Jack and I don't want any part of their money whatsoever.

Mark will sit behind bars until his trial, which will be later this year. We were able to locate the girl Julie who he had been seeing before me and it turns out they definitely did not break up because she moved. Instead, she had moved to get away from Mark. She knew of a girl even before her that we were able to track down as well. All of us have decided to testify, so proving a pattern of behavior is not going to be difficult.

Sometimes I think that they don't need my collaboration in the story and that I could possibly bow out and never have to see him again. But then I remember not only am I doing this for Jack, who needs to be able to say he did the right thing, but I'm doing this for Lisa because she deserves justice. I'm not looking forward to that day in court, but knowing that I have Jack at my side when I do face him and that he will be right there as I tell my story makes everything so much easier.

Jack and I have been talking to Lisa, and it turns out that she had been using the money Jack had been sending to help her local women's shelter. Over the years, she's helped over thirty women get back on their feet with items that they needed such as money for living arrangements, food, and clothes for job interviews. All the things she struggled with when she left Mark.

Somehow, I think knowing that really helped Jack heal. I could see the weight lift off his shoulders from all this and I just know after the trial things are going to be so much different.

"Huckleberry bushes will be ready to pick in about a week," Jack says, pointing to the fruit on the bush along the trail.

We've made it a tradition that at least once a month, but usually more than once, we head up to the cliff. Sadie comes with us and we pack lunch and some snacks for her and we unwind. Sometimes we're so busy we can only carve out an hour. The last time we were here we stayed for three. Without a doubt, this has become our spot.

Once we reach the cliff, we pull out our lunch and give Sadie her bone. She carries it off to the shaded trees behind us where she can still watch us but can enjoy her treat as well.

As we eat, we talk about our plans for the upcoming week, mostly going over how we want to start stocking up and preserving food for winter. He has a hunt planned with Axel. Emelie and I are going to hang out with Cash and Hope while they're gone.

As we pack up the bag once we're done with lunch, he hands me a bottle of water.

"I'll pack this up if you go take Sadie some water. She hasn't had anything to drink since we stopped at the river."

I take the water from him and go over to where Sadie is laying in the shade.

This dog can be as wild as they come and still enjoy all the modern comforts. What's really surprising is she's been trained to drink out of a water bottle. When she's done, I give her a good rub down, and I swear she has the biggest smile on her face as she goes back to her bone.

Turning around to go to where Jack is sitting, my jaw drops. He's down on one knee and holding out a box with the most stunning diamond ring I think I've ever seen.

"I knew that first night when I walked into my cabin and saw you sitting there on the couch in your pajamas that you were someone who was going to be in my life for a while, even though I really tried to fight it. But I knew that day I brought you home from Axel and Emelie's that I wanted to marry you. We just had the matter of getting through the chaos. Even though we still have a fight ahead of us, I'm hoping that you'll do it as my wife and not just as my girlfriend. Will you marry me?" he asks.

I can hear the nerves in his voice. We've talked about marriage but more of an in the future type of thing, so I understand why he's nervous, but he shouldn't be because there's no chance I'd say no.

"Yes, of course, I will." I don't even try to fight the tears in my eyes.

He jumps up and wraps me in a huge hug before slipping the ring on my finger.

Coming out to the middle of nowhere to stay in some guys' cabin I've never met was probably a dumb idea. It was even worse to find out the cabin had been sold, and I was now sitting in a stranger's cabin. But it was the best dumb choice I ever made.

· · · · • · • · · ·

Get Sage and Jack's Bonus epilogue by **joining my newsletter list here.**

Get the next Mountain Men of Whiskey River Book in **Take Me To The Edge.**

Made in the USA
Middletown, DE
02 January 2024

47069636R00066